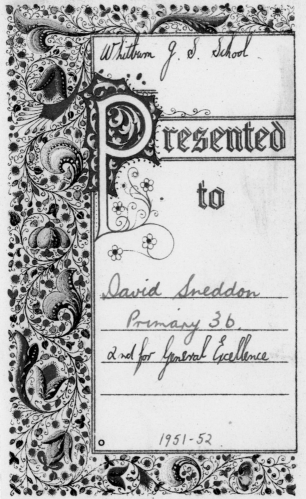

Whitburn J. S. School

Presented to

David Sneddon
Primary 3b.
2nd for General Excellence

1951-52

Charles Burns, 16a Stafford Street, Edinburgh, 3.

MR WHY AND MR WHAT

*

OLD NATURE TALES

GOOD LUCK SERIES

No. 2

" Oh, oh ! " said Blinkie, " Look at Mr. Wikky ! "

(See page 57.)

MR WHY AND MR WHAT

*

OLD NATURE TALES

THOMAS NELSON AND SONS LTD
LONDON EDINBURGH PARIS MELBOURNE
TORONTO AND NEW YORK

THOMAS NELSON AND SONS LTD

Parkside Works Edinburgh 9
3 Henrietta Street London WC2
312 Flinders Street Melbourne C1
5 Parker's Buildings Burg Street Cape Town

THOMAS NELSON AND SONS (CANADA) LTD
91-93 Wellington Street West   Toronto 1

THOMAS NELSON AND SONS
385 Madison Avenue New York 17

SOCIÉTÉ FRANÇAISE D'EDITIONS NELSON
25 rue Henri Barbusse Paris V*

———

First published in this Series 1950

CONTENTS

MR WHY AND MR WHAT

CHAPTER I.

THE NEW ARRIVALS AT WHEREFORE COTTAGE.

" WHAT are little girls made of ?
Sugar and spice and all that's nice;
That's what little girls are made of.

" WHY do they say—
Tell me, pray—
Nice little boys are made of
Slugs and snails
And puppy-dogs' tails ?
That's what little boys are made of."

BLINKIE must have been made of
" sugar and spice and all that's nice,"
because she was a dear little girl.

Her real name was Dorothy Hamilton,
but she was always called Blinkie from
her trick of blinking her eyes when she
asked a question. She asked so many

questions that her nurse would get quite cross with her and say : " It's why, why, why, and what, what, what, all the day long."

So when the little square cottage up the village, which had been empty for years, one morning had the cobwebs cleaned off the windows and the board " To Let " taken down, Blinkie was very pleased.

" Why were the curtains patchwork ? " " What was the use of cutting the hedge when it would grow up again ? " " Why had some one left a packing-case on the lawn ? " And, " What could be in it ? "

She ran to ask Nurse. But Nurse, who was busy, answered snappily,—

" For goodness' sake, go and find out for yourself, and don't worry me with your questions."

Blinkie might be tiresome in asking questions, but she was good and obedient, and always did what she was told. Of

course, Nurse had not really meant her
to go and bother the newcomers, but
Blinkie thought she had.

So she ran through the orchard, which
opened into the lane leading to the square
white cottage.

The name had been painted on the gate.
Although it was growing dark, Blinkie
could spell it out.

"WHEREFORE COTTAGE."

She wished she could catch a glimpse
of the new people before she asked her
questions.

Then some one in the downstairs room
struck a match and lighted a candle. This
the some one placed on the middle of the
table, and as the light stopped flickering
and burned steadily, Blinkie could see all
that was going on inside that room.

Oh, they were funny! They looked
so funny. She laughed to herself. She

had never seen any one quite like them before—not even in her picture-books. They were two old men. She thought they must be brothers. Not that they were at all like each other, but they looked at one another so lovingly.

They sat on opposite sides of the table. One was ever so tall and thin, and the other was ever so short and fat. One had such a mass of white hair, and the other was nearly bald.

Oh, what were they putting on their heads now ? And why were they putting them on ? Funny little black velvet caps with feathers in them. The thin old man had a long feather in his cap, and the fat old man a short one in his cap.

Then, as though they had counted " One, two, three—go ! " they took out those funny feathers and began to scribble, scribble, scribble with them.

What were they writing ? She wished

she knew. She was so curious that she had actually walked through the little gate up the narrow gravel path, and was standing close to the window peeping in.

"Oh!" She jumped back. A brown animal had sprung upon the table. Yes —no—yes, it was—a monkey!

Blinkie began to giggle. The newcomers at Wherefore Cottage were exciting! She pressed her tilted nose against the glass.

The funny old men's lips were moving —the thin one's very quickly, and the fat one's very slowly—while the monkey was chattering as though he too was talking. He lashed his tail so briskly that Blinkie almost cried out, "Mind! you'll upset the inkpot!" Then she remembered that they did not know she was watching, and might send her away if they did.

At last he stopped moving his tail and held it out stiffly in a curve, which reminded Blinkie of the question mark she had made in her copy-book that morning.

Blinkie laughed, not quietly this time, but so loudly that she made quite a noise.

The funny old men stopped writing and looked up. The thin one came to the window.

" Who's there ? Who's there ? " he asked, in his quick voice.

" Me."

Still the thin one could see nobody, for Blinkie had hidden behind a laurel bush.

" Who's Me ? Who's Me ? "

" Blinkie."

She came from behind the bush and stood in front of the window, rather shyly, hanging her head.

" Who is it ? " grunted the fat one, in his big, slow voice.

" A little girl, a little girl," said the thin one, who repeated most of his sentences.

" What does she want ? " the fat one said, also coming over to the window.

" I've come to ask some questions."

" Then you've come to the right—to the right place," the thin one jerked out quickly.

" Have I ? Do lots of people ask you questions ? "

" We answer questions all day long," explained the fat one.

" Do you take it in turns ? "

" Not at all—not at all ! I answer the Whys."

" And I answer the Whats."

" Oh, I see ! " said Blinkie. " You're Mr. Why "—she pointed to the thin old man with her dimpled finger — " and you're Mr. What." She smiled at the fat old man. " The monkey—what does he do ? "

The two old men nodded at one another.

" We'll show you what he does."

They said something to the monkey, who with a grin bounded out of the room, opened the front door, and poked his head round it.

He must be their servant. Oh, what a funny pair they were, to have a monkey for a servant !

The monkey had opened the door so that she might go in.

She followed him into the parlour. Mr. Why and Mr. What were again writing. Between them was a high stool, to which the monkey pointed. Blinkie climbed on to it, while the brown animal sprang back on the table.

She turned to Mr. What and said,—

" Why do you have patchwork curtains ? "

Was he deaf, and had not heard ? He did not answer.

She asked the question again. Still

there was no answer. Then Mr. Why
put down his pen. So Blinkie turned
to him.

" I am afraid your brother can't hear
me very well. I have asked him twice
why you have patchwork curtains, but he
has not answered."

" You must ask me the Whys and him
the Whats, Little Dear, Little Dear."

" We have patchwork curtains because
my brother wanted green and I wanted
yellow, and the Wicked One wanted red
to match his coat. So we made them all
colours, all colours, to please every one."

" The Wicked One ? " said Blinkie.
" You mean the monkey ? Why do you
call him the Wicked One ? "

" Because he's so naughty, so naughty,"
explained Mr. Why.

" Some folk call him Wikky for short,"
grunted Mr. What, looking fondly at the
monkey, while Mr. Why patted his head.

(4,699)

" Why do you have patchwork curtains? "

See page 15.

They both seemed to love him very much.

" And why do you cut down the yew hedge when it will grow up again ? "

" Because when it grows too tall it keeps the sunlight out of the room."

" Oh, I see ! "

And then, shyly, because she was afraid it might be rude,—

" What— Oh, but I must ask your brother the Whats." She turned to the fat old man. " What is the use of those funny little caps on your heads ? "

" To hold our quill pens. If we leave them on the table the Wicked One hides them, and then we cannot get on with our work."

What Blinkie had thought were feathers were quill pens.

" And *what* . . . is in the big wooden case on the lawn outside ? "

Mr. What smiled.

" All the questions we have to answer, Miss Blinkie. If you will come again some day and see us, we will tell you some of them."

" Oh, thank you ever so much," said Blinkie.

" She's a little dear, a little dear," said Mr. Why, patting one hand fondly.

" Good-bye, Miss Blinkie," said Mr. What, patting the other.

The Wicked One sprang off the table to open the door, grinning from ear to ear, and winking his eye as much as to say, " I'm glad you're a girl, not a boy. Of course, I don't believe all that silly nonsense about little girls being made of sugar and spice, and little boys being made of slugs and snails. But little boys are rough, and make faces at me and pull my tail. So I am glad you are a little girl, and you can come as often as you like to Wherefore Cottage."

CHAPTER II.

MR. WHY TELLS THE LITTLE DEAR ABOUT PANCAKE DAY.

" And every man and maid do take their turn,
And toss the pancake up for fear it burn."

BLINKIE wished very much to go and see those funny old men again. She wanted to see the monkey—dear Mr. Wikky, who looked at her with his head on one side, as though he understood everything she said.

One sunny morning she was swinging in the orchard, in a clean pink cotton frock and a clean pink cotton sunbonnet. Up, up she swung. Then down, down. Up, up again. Snatch !

" Oh ! " shrieked Blinkie, and nearly

fell out of the swing, because she put her hand up so quickly to her head.

Her sunbonnet ! What had happened to it ? It had suddenly been torn off her head. It must have caught on one of the branches of the apple tree.

She jumped out of the swing and looked up. Between the boughs she could see something pink, and yet it was moving about and jumping. Underneath it was something brown.

Was it—could it be ? She stood on tiptoe gazing up. The pink bonnet and the brown object underneath it leapt across from bough to bough. It was—it was the Wicked One !

The monkey ran up to the top of the tree, where it sat playing with the strings, tying them, untying them, taking off the bonnet, putting it on again.

" Give me my bonnet ! " shrieked Blinkie. " Give me my bonnet ! "

The Wicked One grinned at her. He swung himself down, pulling the clean bonnet after him through the leaves of the apple tree.

He stood before Blinkie, and just as she expected him to hand her the bonnet, with a bow he turned, put it on his head, and ran through the long grass, out of the orchard gate, and up the lane.

" Mr. Wikky, Mr. Wikky, my bonnet ! " cried Blinkie, running after him.

There was no stopping the monkey. Once or twice, when she thought she had caught him, he darted away again ; and it was not until she reached the garden of Wherefore Cottage that she got near enough to him to snatch it back.

Then she looked up and saw her old friends sitting in the garden. Mr. Why was perched on a high stool, under a very tall green umbrella striped with red. Mr.

What was seated on a low stool, under a red umbrella covered with green spots, which was so low that you could hardly see his head underneath it.

What were they doing ?

Blinkie went up to them, and, peeping between the two umbrellas, had a good look.

They were busy writing—Mr. Why on very big paper, very quickly ; and Mr. What on very little paper, very slowly.

Then Blinkie saw something which made her cry out,—

" Why do you have your ink in a soup-tureen ? "

Mr. Why looked up.

" It's the Little Dear, the Little Dear. —Come and sit here, and I will tell you."

Blinkie sat down on the grass under Mr. Why's tall umbrella.

" We have our ink in a soup-tureen because we have so much writing to do.

People send us questions to answer all day long."

Blinkie jumped up to watch Mr. Why writing on the big sheets of paper.

She wrinkled her forehead.

" You write everything twice over ? " she said.

" Yes, yes," said Mr. Why. " I write so much more quickly than Mr. What that, unless I write everything twice over, I should answer twice the number of questions that he does."

" Oh ! " said Blinkie. " Is that why you say so many of your words twice over ? "

" That's it ! that's it ! " said Mr. Why. " I talk so much more quickly than my brother that, unless I spoke some of my words twice over, I should speak many more in the day than he does."

" P-a-n-c-a-k-e D-a-y ! " Blinkie spelt out. " Why are you writing about Pancake Day ? "

Peeping between the two umbrellas. *See page 23.*

" Some one has written to ask me why we eat pancakes on Shrove Tuesday."

" Please tell me," coaxed Blinkie. " We always have pancakes at home on Shrove Tuesday."

Blinkie sat down once more at Mr. Why's feet, but a second later she was up again.

" Where's Mr. Wikky gone ? I am sure he likes pancakes." He had been there a moment ago. " Mr. Wikky—Wikky ! " she called.

Next minute she saw the Wicked One come leaping out of the house holding something behind his back.

" Mr. Wikky," said Blinkie, " come and sit beside me. We're going to hear a story."

The Wicked One sat down and held up over Blinkie's head a walking stick, making believe it was an umbrella.

As the little girl sat with her arm round

the monkey listening to Mr. Why's story, Mr. What went on writing busily, making his "o's" very big and round, and crossing all his "t's" so carefully that the cross bits did not go up and down like Blinkie's did, but were as straight as a ruler.

" To eat pancakes on Shrove Tuesday is a very old custom," said Mr. Why. " It is hundreds and hundreds of years old. Once upon a time, in all the big towns and all the little villages, early on Shrove Tuesday morning a bell used to be rung. It was called the ' Pancake Bell,' and as soon as it sounded all the folk would run into the kitchens and toss the pancakes for fear they should burn. The man or maid who burnt a pancake, or let one fall to the ground, was sure to lose something he was very fond of before the year was out."

" Oh dear ! " said Blinkie ; " they are

so easy to drop. When cook let me toss a pancake I dropped it on the floor. Oh, and I remember now. I lost my gold brooch the next week, the one made like a wish-bone with a pearl in it that Uncle Henry gave me at Christmas. Next time I toss pancakes I shall have to be ever so careful."

CHAPTER III.

THE FIRST EASTER EGG.

" Mother Hen sings,
  As she flaps her wings :
    ' Cluckety-cluckety-cluck.
  For some little maid
  An egg I've laid—
    Chuckety-chuckety-chuck.' "

ON Shrove Tuesday Blinkie had helped Cook to toss the pancakes. Now Lent was near an end. Good Friday had come, and Blinkie was eating her hot cross bun. But, alas ! poor Blinkie had caught a cold and was very hoarse. She felt sad, because she knew it meant hot lemon-and-water in bed, which she hated, and being kept in the nursery for several days for fear she should get into a draught and make it worse.

There was something else, though, which bothered her. She felt certain she was going to think of some question she would want to ask the funny old men, and would not be able to do so.

Sure enough, on Easter morning, she did! On the chest of drawers was a big chocolate Easter egg.

"Oh," said Blinkie when she looked at it, smelt it, nibbled off a tiny corner of the edge, "I wonder why——"

She stopped. It would not be any use asking Nurse. She would not know. If only—if only she had been able to go to Wherefore Cottage, she could have asked Mr. Why to tell her why little boys and little girls are given Easter eggs on Easter Sunday.

But there was no chance of her being

allowed out. Her cold was worse, and it was a damp, rainy day.

Why—why did you have Easter eggs ? She could not read her book, nor think of anything to do. Oh dear ! why had she got this nasty cold ? It was *too, too* tiresome. Even the Easter egg was spoiled now, because every time she looked at it she remembered the question she so badly wanted to ask. What did other little boys and girls do, she wondered, who were not so lucky as to live close to Wherefore Cottage ?

Blinkie had been sitting on the broad window-seat swinging her legs, and watching the rain patter, patter on the glass.

She started up. She knew ! They wrote. That big crate she had seen on the lawn was full of letters they had written. Why should she not write ? Mummie would pass the cottage on the

way to church. She would leave the
note.

Blinkie no longer felt dull. She had
something to do.

She fetched her pink notepaper, and
sitting down at the big nursery table,
wrote :—

    " DEAR, DARLING MR. WHY,—

        " Please do tell me why little boys
and girls are given Easter eggs on Easter
Sunday.

    " Lots of love and kisses from

                " BLINKIE."

When the letter was finished Mummie
took it, and said she would bring the
answer on the way back from church.

Oh dear, what an awful lot of sermon
they must be having ! The clock had
struck twelve a long time ago. Would
Mummie never come back ?

Then she heard her mother's voice in the hall, and barely two minutes later the nursery door opened and Mummie's pretty golden head came round the corner.

" I've brought the answer, darling," she said.

Only it wasn't a note. It was something ever so much better. It was Mr. Why himself !

Oh, Blinkie was surprised and pleased !

" Mr. Why ! Mr. Why ! " She danced up to him, and he bent his long back and said,—

" So the poor Little Dear, the poor Little Dear has a bad, bad cold."

He stood his tall umbrella in the corner, and hung his waterproof cape on the back of the door.

" The Little Dear, the Little Dear wants to ask me a question ? "

He sat down in the big armchair on

one side of the fire, holding out his hands to the nice red blaze. Blinkie sat on her little stool on the other, her fingers clasped round her knees.

" I want to know ever so badly," she said, " why little boys and little girls are given Easter eggs on Easter Sunday."

Mr. Why smiled softly. A far-away look came into his blue eyes.

" It's a beautiful story—a very beautiful story, Little Dear." He spoke in a solemn voice.

Then he told it.

" Once there lived a poor old man. He was very good and holy, and read his Bible and said his prayers every day. But there were wicked men and women in the village, who not only did not read their Bibles and say their prayers them-selves, but were angry that the old man did so; for they did not believe in God.

"So they came to his cottage and told him that, if he would not say that he too did not believe in God, they would imprison him in a loft, and leave him there to starve to death.

"The old man was far too good to say he did not believe in God if he did. So they took him and locked him up in the loft, into which only a tiny ray of light could creep through a crack in the roof. They gave him neither straw to sleep on nor food to eat. Every morning his jailers came to him and said, ' Do you believe in God ? ' And he always answered, ' I believe.'

"It was Easter morning. The poor old man was now so frail and ill that the wicked men were quite sure he could not live through the day unless he had food to eat.

"They came to him early in the morning and said,—

" ' If you will only say you do not believe in God, we will let you free and give you food.'

" ' I believe in God, so I will not say I do not. I would rather die to-day.' His voice was so weak that the wicked folk could barely hear his words.

" ' Let him starve ! let him starve ! ' they said as they went off singing and shouting and making a great noise.

" Their footsteps had barely died away when the old man, who was lying in a corner with his hands over his eyes, heard the fluttering of wings, and, looking up, saw on the ground beside him a beautiful white hen. The first thing he thought was : How could the hen have got into the loft ? for the door was bolted outside, and the crack in the roof was far too small to have let in a sparrow, to say nothing of a large bird such as this ?

" The hen got up and began to strut

On the ground beside him a beautiful white hen.

See page 36.

about, cluck-clucking, and the old man saw on the ground a large brown egg.

" ' A beautiful, beautiful egg ! ' He looked up to thank the bird for its help, but it had gone.

" Every morning the same thing happened. The Easter hen came—how, the old man knew not—and when it had laid the brown egg it flew away.

" Each morning the wicked jailers came and expected to find the old man dead ; but they saw to their surprise that his face was growing fatter and his voice stronger every day. It seemed as though somebody must be giving him food. But who could it be, since they held the key of the door ?

" So one of them agreed to stay in the loft with the old man, and watch if he was being helped.

" The jailer had barely settled himself in a corner before he too heard the rush

of wings and saw the white hen. Then
he saw the egg. He looked for the hen
again, but it had gone.

" He was so frightened at what he had
seen that he ran out and told the others.
They came back to the loft and asked the
old man, who told them about the visit
of the Easter hen. They thought a lot
about what he had said, and made up
their minds God must love those who
believe in Him very much, when He
cared for them as He had cared for the
holy old man.

" So in that little village the story of
the Easter hen was handed down, and
it became the custom of the mothers
to give their children eggs on Easter
Sunday, to remind them how God
cares for those He loves and who love
Him."

When Mr. Why finished speaking there
was a silence in the nursery.

" I think," said Blinkie slowly, " it is a very nice story."

" Yes, Little Dear; yes, Little Dear," said Mr. Why slowly, and Blinkie thought she saw him wipe some tears out of his faded blue eyes. " It is indeed a very beautiful, a very beautiful story."

CHAPTER IV.

THE OLD MEN GO A-MAYING WITH SOME YOUNG FOLK.

> " The moon shines bright,
> And the stars give a light
> A little before it is day ;
> So God bless you all,
> Both great and small,
> And send you a joyful May."

WHEN the first of May came Blinkie was well again. Because it was such a bright morning and the sun was shining so warmly, she was sent to play in the garden.

When she was tired of skipping, and had given her dolly a ride in the pram as far as the orchard gate, she drew it up beneath the pear tree, and scrambled up on to the wall to see who was coming along in the farm cart she could hear down the lane.

It was Farmer Gibbs.

Oh, his horse ! Its mane and tail were tied up with ribbons and flowers and twists of straw. Why was it so gay ? She was almost afraid to ask him, because he was such a cross old man. Still, she screwed up her courage.

" Please, Farmer Gibbs," she called in her pretty voice, " why has your horse got all those ribbons on him ? Is it his birthday ? "

" For certain no," Farmer Gibbs answered.

" Then why is he looking like that ? "

" Doesn't ye know what to-day is ? " snarled the farmer.

Blinkie shook her head.

" Then the sooner ye finds out the better."

He had answered so crossly that Blinkie

was glad when the cart passed round the corner.

" Then you had better find out," she repeated. She would find out. She would run and ask her old friends, who were never grumpy, no matter how many questions she asked them.

So, jumping down and running the pram before her, she hurried along the road to Wherefore Cottage.

No sooner had she reached the gate than she called out,—

" Mr. Why, Mr. What ! Where are you ? I want to ask you each a question dreadful quick."

" Coming down, Little Dear, coming down," came from one room upstairs.

" Just putting my letters tidy," came from the other room upstairs.

A minute later Mr. Why came out of the front door. Blinkie rushed at him.

" I've just seen Farmer Gibbs's horse,

and I want to know why its mane and
tail are tied up with ribbons and flowers
and bits of straw."

Before Mr. Why had time to answer,
Mr. What came waddling down the stairs.

" Oh, and there's Mr. What ! What is
to-day ?   Farmer Gibbs said if I didn't
know the sooner I found out the better."

" It's May Day, for sure," said Mr.
What.

" And Farmer Gibbs's horse, Farmer
Gibbs's horse is gay with ribbons because
it's the first of May," Mr. Why joined
in.   " Once all the horses were gay with
ribbons.   In olden times folk went a-
Maying on the first of May just as much
as we keep Christmas on the twenty-fifth
of December nowadays."

" Oh, it must have been fun to go a-
Maying.   Did they have games and romps
and dance around the Maypole ? "

" That's it, that's it," said Mr. Why.

" The folk went into the woods and chose the fairest maiden for the May Queen. They picked boughs of may and presented them to her, and crowned her with a garland. The village lads made believe they were Robin Hood, Will Stukeley, Friar Tuck, and such merry men. They shot with arrows at a popinjay, which is, Little Dear, Little Dear, a target made in the shape of a bird."

" Oh ! " said Blinkie. " I wish I'd lived then ! " She took hold of Mr. Why's hand. " Oh, Mr. Why," she said, " couldn't we make believe we lived ever so long ago ? "

" In the reign of Henry VIII., in the reign of Henry VIII.," laughed Mr. Why, entering into the game.

" Never was a king so fond of Maying as Henry VIII.," added Mr. What.

" Oh yes," said Blinkie, " let's make believe we are living in the reign of

Henry VIII., and are going a-Maying because it's the first of May."

" Wait a minute, wait a minute," said Mr. Why. He nodded at Mr. What, and Mr. What nodded back at Mr. Why. " You sit there, Little Dear, Little Dear, till we come down again."

So Blinkie sat on the lawn while the two old men went indoors.

She wondered what they were doing, and felt sure it was something very exciting. Then she remembered she had not seen the Wicked One that morning.

The thought had barely come to her when he appeared, rolling in front of him a large bundle, which he tossed on to her lap. He ran away grinning and chattering.

She opened it, and took out a blue-and-white frock such as a little girl of her own age might have worn in the days of

King Henry VIII. There was a blue velvet cap as well.

She slipped the frock over her pink overall. She took off her sunbonnet and pushed the cap over her golden curls. Oh, she wished she could see herself!

She was running indoors to find a mirror when she stopped in surprise. A gallant figure was coming down the stairs. It was—oh, such a fat man! He was wearing a beautiful velvet and silk suit, and a hat with a long pink plume in it.

"Oh!" she screamed. Then she danced with joy. "It's Mr. What! and you're dressed up to be Henry VIII."

Behind Mr. What came Mr. Why in a suit of huntsman's green. Last of all came the Wicked One. But, oh, what a figure of fun he looked! He was dressed in a little satin suit with lace ruffles, and a three-cornered hat many sizes too big for him. Round his neck was a tray, on which were piled real gingerbread cakes.

" What is Mr. Wikky ? " said Blinkie, gathering up her long skirts.

" He's Tiddy - Doll," answered Mr. Why. " No May-Day revels were ever complete without old Tiddy. Although he only sold gingerbread, he wore fine clothes ; so it has become a well-known saying, ' to be as fine as Tiddy-Doll.' "

The Mayers went out on to the lawn.

" Now," said Mr. Why, pulling the garden seat forward, " the first thing we must do is to choose a May Queen."

" Y-yes," said Blinkie. " You haven't chosen one yet, have you ? "

" The king, the king must choose the May Queen," said Mr. Why to Mr. What.

Fat King Henry VIII. waved his plumed hat.

" We choose Miss Blinkie for our May Queen."

"Oh, Mr. Wikky, take care, or you'll spill them all!"

See page 50.

" Fancy choosing me! " she said, with delight.

She felt most important when Henry VIII. lifted her on to the garden seat, and his huntsman, breaking a branch of pink may from the tree which grew on the edge of the lawn, made it into a wreath, that his royal master might crown her.

The Wicked One bowed in front of her until his gingerbreads slid along the tray, and the Queen had to call out,—

" Oh, Mr. Wikky, take care, or you'll spill them all ! "

" Now," said the huntsman, when Blinkie had been crowned Queen of the May, " I command, I command Robin Hood and his men to appear and take part in the shooting contest."

" But," said the Queen of the May, and there were tears in her eyes, " there is no Robin Hood, nor Will Stukeley, nor Friar Tuck. Whatever shall we do ? "

The sound of boyish laughter came echoing down the lane.

" It's the Vicarage boys ! " said Blinkie, starting up.

She got up on to the seat to see over the hedge.

" It's Rob and William, and Podgy their fat cousin. Rob for Robin, William for Will Stukeley, Fat Podgy for fat Friar Tuck. It couldn't be better. May I call them into the garden, Mr. What, and ask them to be our bowmen ? "

Mr. Why, however, was already at the gate putting green caps on their heads, bows and arrows into their hands, and inviting them to come and join in King Henry VIII.'s May-Day revels.

He pointed to the Wicked One, who had been as good as the gingerbreads, but at the sight of boys on his lawn was not looking so sweet-tempered.

" When, when you have shot your arrows at the popinjay you shall eat as much, as much gingerbread as you can," said Mr. Why, in his kind old way.

This pleased the boys very much, for all three were fond of gingerbread, most of all the podgy cousin.

The popinjay which Mr. What had fetched out of the cottage was placed against the yew hedge. The boys were eager for the fun.

" . . . Splendid, splendid ! " said Mr. Why, as Friar Tuck took aim and his arrow hit the bird's beak.

" Now it's my turn," said Robin.

His arrow flew through the air, and struck the bird's tail.

The last to shoot was Will Stukeley.

He was the smallest of the three, and Blinkie did hope he would win.

Mr. Why and Mr. What shaded their eyes with their hands.

" He's hit the bird on the wing," cried the Queen of the May.

Forgetful of her royal dignity she jumped off the seat, and, running to Will Stukeley, flung her arms about his neck and gave him a kiss.

" You've all done very well, very well," said the royal huntsman.

" Yes," said his royal master. " England can fear no foe while her sons can shoot so true."

The fat cousin thought it was now time for the gingerbread.

" Tiddy-Doll—" he began. He looked round. " He was here a minute **ago**. Where's he gone ? "

Every one looked. No one could see the naughty Tiddy-Doll.

It was half an hour later that they came across him. The old men were looking in the attic ; Blinkie was hunting in the kitchen cupboard.

It was the Vicarage boys who found him.
Rob saw the tip of a brown tail coming
from underneath the mulberry tree.

" There's the bounder ! " he cried.

" And what's he doing ? " screamed
Will.

" 'Pon my word ! " shouted Friar Tuck
in disgust, as he parted the leaves, " if
he hasn't eaten every crumb of **gingerbread !** "

The three boys rushed at Mr. Wikky
to pull his tail and pinch his ears, and
show him what they thought of his greed.

The Wicked One knew what was coming.

Up the tree he scrambled, and sat on
the top branch, looking down at those
boys he hated so much, still munching
the last crumbs of the tasty gingerbread.

CHAPTER V.

BLINKIE'S OLD FRIENDS FORETELL STORMY WEATHER.

" Red sky in the morning
Is shepherd's warning."

BLINKIE was very excited. Sunday was her birthday. On Friday evening, when her mother came and tucked her up in bed, she told her she might have a picnic ; but as her birthday was on Sunday, she must have her party on Saturday or Monday. She could ask any friends she liked.

Blinkie chose Saturday, because it came before Monday.

" Please, Mummie, I want Mr. Why, Mr. What, and Mr. Wikky."

At breakfast the following morning the sky looked gray ; but Daddy said,—

" It is often the cloudy morning that turns out the brightest day, and it is more than likely that the sun will be shining by twelve o'clock."

As soon as she was told that she might leave the table, she ran to Wherefore Cottage to invite her guests to picnic with her in Hurst Woods that afternoon.

When she reached the gate she stopped, surprised. Mr. Why, Mr. What, and the Wicked One were coming out of the house ready dressed for a walk.

The old men were wrapped in big waterproof capes, and each held an umbrella over his head. The Wicked One walked behind with a conceited swagger, his tail very upright, for tied on to the end of it was Mr. Why's check mackintosh spongebag, and strapped on to his head was Mr. What's big round sponge.

" Oh, oh ! " said Blinkie, stopping in front of them. " Look at Mr. Wikky ! Why has he got a sponge on his head, and a sponge-bag on his tail ? "

" To catch the raindrops, the raindrops," said Mr. Why.

" He likes to wash in rain-water, Miss Blinkie," joined in Mr. What.

The Wicked One nodded his head so often that the sponge slipped over one eye.

" But it isn't going to rain."

" Yes, it is, Miss Blinkie—going to rain very fast."

" That's why, that's why we are taking our waterproofs and our umbrellas."

Blinkie's face fell.

" But Daddy said he thought the sun would shine by twelve o'clock, and I want it to be fine so badly because I am having a picnic this afternoon. You see it's my birthday to-morrow, so Mother said

I must have my party on Saturday or Monday. I have come to ask you both and Mr. Wikky to have tea with me in Hurst Woods. I have chosen you three for my birthday guests."

When the Wicked One heard about the party he jumped for joy. He ran up to Blinkie, clapped his paws, grinned, put his head first on one side then on the other, smacked his lips, and patted his chest as much as to say, " Birthday cake ! Mr. Wikky is the boy for birthday cake ! "

But Mr. Why and Mr. What shook their heads.

" Kind little girl, kind little girl," said Mr. Why.

" Thank you, Miss Blinkie," said Mr. What.

Then they both said together,—

" But we want you to choose Monday for the picnic, because it's going to rain this afternoon."

" Why are you so certain it's going to rain ? " pouted Blinkie.

Mr. Why took one of Blinkie's hands in his ; Mr. What took the other.

" We will show you—" said Mr. What.

" Why we know it's going to rain," joined in Mr. Why.

They led her on to the lawn in front of Wherefore Cottage, the Wicked One following them with the sponge-bag dragging across the grass. Then they stopped, and Mr. What raised his fat first finger.

" What do you hear, Miss Blinkie ? "

Blinkie screwed up her forehead and listened. The Wicked One put one paw behind his ear.

" I can only hear the geese cackling," said Blinkie, " and the sheep bleating, and the frogs croaking."

Mr. What patted her hand, and Mr. Why squeezed her fingers as he explained.

" Those are some of the reasons why
we know it is going to rain."

" Yes, Miss Blinkie," put in Mr. What.
" When the geese cackle, and the sheep
bleat, and the frogs croak, it is a sure
sign the rain is not an hour away."

" And there is going to be rain and
wind, and wind and rain," shivered Mr.
Why—" so violent, so wild, that the dogs
will run into the cottages and lie asleep
before the fire."

" Ugh ! " shuddered the Wicked One,
as he hid under the folds of Mr. What's
waterproof cape.

" How do you know it is going to rain
and wind so dreadfully much ? " asked
Blinkie.

Once again Mr. What raised his finger.

" Listen, Miss Blinkie. What do you
hear now ? "

" A bird singing," Blinkie answered.

" That's the missel thrush," Mr. What

"Oh," said Binkie, "the hens are funny."

See page 62.

explained. " And bad weather always follows when the missel thrush sings loudly. His other name is the storm-cock."

Then Mr. What moved off the lawn, and told Blinkie to follow him.

He went to the back of Wherefore Cottage. Over the wooden fence was a big farmyard. He lifted Blinkie in his arms so that she could peep over the top of the palings.

" Tell me, Miss Blinkie, what you can see."

" Oh," said Blinkie, " the hens are funny. They are having dust-baths. There's an ugly fat pig in the corner trying to play, rolling over, falling down, getting up. Does he ever stop still ? "

" Not when it's going to rain," said Mr. What. " Those are two more signs of rain—hens rolling in the dust and the pigs never stopping still."

Mr. What was about to lift Blinkie

down when she clung to the top of the palings.

" Wait a minute, wait a minute ! " she cried. " Mr. Wikky's got into the farm-yard. What is he doing ? "

The Wicked One was running after a cloud of feathers which were blowing in front of him.

" Yet another sign of wet weather, to see the feathers blowing," said Mr. What, as the naughty monkey scrambled up the fence with a long chicken's feather stuck into the sponge, just like a feather in a hat.

Then Mr. Why came round the back of Wherefore Cottage, and told Blinkie to come with him. So she trotted after the tall old man into the kitchen.

" Oh," she said, drawing back, " the spiders ! Why are there so many spiders on the walls ? "

" Because it's going to be very rainy,

Little Dear; because it's going to be very rainy."

When they came out of Wherefore Cottage they could not see Mr. What anywhere. The Wicked One was dancing on one foot, and holding on to the other with his paw.

" Why," said Blinkie, looking up at Mr. Why, " is Mr. Wikky doing that ? Has he hurt his foot ? "

" It is his corns, his corns," said Mr. Why. " They always hurt him when the rain is coming."

" Now I remember," said Blinkie, " Nurse had dreadful bad corns this morning, and they made her so cross. I shall always know when Nurse has bad corns that rain is coming."

The Wicked One was in such pain that Mr. Why picked him up, put him on his shoulder, and took him indoors to find some corn plaster.

Blinkie was left alone in the porch. She looked round. Where was Mr. What ? Where could he be ?

On the other side of the mulberry tree, whose leaves were so thick that they almost hid the flower-bed beyond it from the cottage, she caught a glimpse of her fat old friend. He was bending over a bunch of yellow blooms.

What was he doing ? She ran across to him.

" What a lazy flower ! " she said, as she saw that he was looking at a marigold whose petals were tightly closed. " It is not awake yet."

Mr. What smiled. He spoke slowly, in his old-fashioned way.

" The petals of the marigold are still closed," he said, " because the rain is at hand. Dear little marigold. It is such a pretty story. I am so fond of it."

" Tell me, please," coaxed Blinkie.

(4,699)

5

There was a wheelbarrow on the path.
Mr. What sat on it, and Blinkie clam-
bered up to his knee. " I love a pretty
story."

" Once upon a time," said Mr. What,
" the Moon and the Sun were each asked
to give a present to poor, dark, cold Earth.
The Moon gave the Evening Primrose,
and the Sun gave the Marigold. The
Marigold, however, was timid, and felt
lonely in the cold big world. So the Sun
promised to come every morning and kiss
her and wake her up. When the rain is
coming you will always find the petals of
the Marigold closed, because the sun cannot get through the clouds to open her
eyes. Last night I knew the Marigold
would be asleep to-day, for the Sun went
to bed pale, and the clouds in the sky
were like wild horsemen. When I woke
up this morning the sky in the east was
red.

' Red sky in the morning
Is shepherd's warning,' "

repeated Mr. What, who was fond of quoting verses of poetry.

" I don't think," said Blinkie, with her eyes still fixed on the sleeping marigold, " I shall have my picnic after all to-day."

She was glad she had put off the picnic, for as she reached the orchard gate the first drops of rain began to fall; and she had to run quickly indoors, because, not being as wise as the funny old men and their monkey friend, she had no water-proof cape or mackintosh sponge-bag to keep her dry.

CHAPTER VI.

MR. WHY AND MR. WHAT PROMISE BLINKIE A FINE DAY FOR HER PICNIC.

" Red sky at night
Is shepherd's delight."

BLINKIE jumped out of bed early on Monday morning. She ran to the window and raised the blind to see if it would be fine for her picnic.

Dear, dear! The sun was not up yet. How could she tell whether it would be wet or fine? If only she could ask her old friends! She knew that hens rolled in the dust and the missel thrush sang when rain was coming, but she had never thought of asking either Mr. What or

Something was scratching, scratching on the window.

 See page 70.

Mr. Why how she could tell if it would be fine. They would be sure to know.

She went back to bed and shut her eyes; but she could not sleep, for the ravens were croaking so loudly in the trees.

What was that? What was it? Something was scratching, scratching on the window.

Blinkie sat up, and saw the Wicked One grinning at her through the glass.

Oh, how lucky it was that he had come! Perhaps he would be able to tell if it was going to be a fine afternoon.

Blinkie opened the window to let in the monkey. He sprang on to the washstand-rail, where he sat twisting the fringe of the towel into knots.

" Oh, you mustn't do that, you naughty Mr. Wikky ! " protested Blinkie. " Nurse will think I have done it, and be so angry with me that perhaps she will not let me have a picnic after all. Oh, dear Mr. Wikky, can you tell me if it will be fine for my party ? "

Blinkie waited anxiously.

Mr. Wikky shook his head. He did not know. He chattered and grinned wickedly. He sprang off the washstand-rail, turned head over heels into Blinkie's warm bed, pulling up the snug eider-down round his neck tightly, so as not to let in any draughts.

He pointed from Blinkie through the open window to Wherefore Cottage. Next he snuggled down so that he could not be seen, breathed heavily, even snored a little, and sometimes turned just like she did when she was having exciting dreams.

Blinkie knew what he meant.

Oh, it was a lovely idea ! She was to go to Wherefore Cottage and ask Mr. Why and Mr. What to tell her the weather signs for a fine day, while Mr. Wikky stayed in her bed and made believe he was she in case Nurse peeped in.

It was only six o'clock, and it would not take her five minutes to run to Wherefore Cottage. She would be back in bed again long before Nurse came to dress her.

She put on her blue dressing-gown, and pushed her pink dimpled feet into her fluffy blue bedroom slippers. She opened the door gently, and crept down the broad oak staircase.

She opened the window in the hall, passed through, and closed it behind her. There was a winding path through the orchard, and Blinkie walked along it, for the grass was white with dew.

There was no one in the lane. The hedges looked so pretty, covered with floating cobwebs.

When she reached the gate of Wherefore Cottage she stopped. She looked up.

The patchwork curtains were drawn over the windows.

"Oh dear ! she had never thought of that. How stupid of her ! Her funny old friends were still asleep. She could not knock on the door and wake them up just to ask if it was going to be fine that afternoon, because they might be vexed with her. Suppose Mr. Why and Mr. What did not get up till eight o'clock. Long before then Nurse would have found Mr. Wikky. It would be funny if she took him out of bed and put him in her bath and dressed him in her clothes, for Nurse was absent-minded sometimes.

Blinkie began to laugh. Fancy the monkey sitting in her place at breakfast, and Mummie saying, " Now, Blinkie darling, we are all waiting to start. Say your grace."

She was still laughing when the curtains of the room on the left-hand side of

the porch, and the curtains of the room
on the right-hand side of the porch, were
drawn back at the same moment, and Mr.
Why's head, in a violet nightcap with a
scarlet tassel, appeared at one window, and
Mr. What's head, in a scarlet nightcap with
a violet tassel, appeared at the other.

Then Mr. Why put up his hand to his
ear, and Mr. What put up his hand to
shade his eyes.

" Listen ! " said the former.

" Look ! " said the latter. They nodded
their heads until they almost nodded off
the tassels.

" Yes," said Mr. What. " I hear the
ravens croaking in the trees."

" And I see the dew, the dew on the
grass, even from here," said Mr. Why.

Then they both leaned far out of the
windows, and craned their necks to look
up to the roof.

" Is the smoke—" began Mr. What.

" Yes, yes," said Mr. Why; " it is rising straight from the chimney."

Whereupon they both exclaimed together,—

" So it will be a fine day for the picnic ! "

" Oh, oh ! " called Blinkie, running through the gate, standing on the path, and looking up at the two heads coming out of the two windows. " Does it mean it is going to be a fine day when the ravens croak loudly and there is lots of dew on the grass ? "

" Why, it's the Little Dear, the Little Dear ! " said Mr. Why.

" Whatever is Miss Blinkie doing out of doors so early ? " said Mr. What.

" I wanted to know if it was going to be fine this afternoon," Blinkie exclaimed, " so I came down to ask you about the weather. When I got here I thought you were both asleep. I was just going away when you pulled back the curtains and looked out."

" Last night," said Mr. What, " we felt sure it would be fine for your picnic to-day."

" What made you think so ? "

> " Red sky at night ·
> Is shepherd's delight,"

quoted Mr. What, who recited the poetry bits ; while Mr. Why told the long stories to save time, because he talked so much more quickly than his brother.

" Last evening, Little Dear, Little Dear," said Mr. Why, " the wind shifted to the east."

He pointed with his long, thin finger across the tree-tops to the tall church spire with the golden weathercock on the steeple.

Now Mr. What recited another dear little verse.—

" The South wind often brings wet weather,
The North wind, wet and cold together;
The West wind always brings us rain,
The East wind blows it back again."

" The swallows were flying high, so high," added Mr. Why. " The bat was flying late, so late."

" The gnats were so thick in the garden," grunted Mr. What, " that we had to send the Wicked One with a fan to fan them away."

" Does all that mean," said Blinkie, " that fine weather is coming ? "

" Surely, surely," said Mr. Why.

" And when you came down the lane," asked Mr. What, " were the cobwebs floating on the hedges ? "

" Yes," said Blinkie, " heaps of them. I thought how pretty they looked."

She had barely finished her sentence when the sun began to shine. It shone so brightly upon the silver dew and upon her golden curls that the farmer's boy who went by with the milk blinked his eyes, and said he had seen a fairy in the garden of Wherefore Cottage.

" It's—it's going to be a lovely day ! " cried Blinkie, clapping her hands.

" Croak-croak ! " went the ravens, so loudly that she had to raise her voice.

" You won't be late ? You'll come quite by four. There's to be strawberry jam and birthday cake."

She blew a kiss to Mr. Why and Mr. What.

" I must go now, or else Nurse will find I am out, and be angry."

She was about to tell them how she had tucked the Wicked One into her bed when the patchwork curtains were drawn again, and as she turned away she heard a loud snore coming from the room on the right, and a loud snore coming from the room on the left.

She ran all the way home, and hurrying up the oak stairs, slipped back into her night nursery.

One minute later, before she was able to change places with the Wicked One, she heard a step outside and saw the handle turn. It was Nurse !

Mr. Wikky lay cuddled up in bed, underneath the sheets. Blinkie slipped behind the wardrobe. Her heart was beating quickly. Would Nurse be very angry ?

Nurse came into the room. She stopped and looked towards the bed.

" There, now . . . the lazy little girl . . . not awake yet ! "

She moved towards the bed.

" Oh dear ! " thought Blinkie, and held her breath.

But Nurse had turned away.

" She was late to bed last night. I'll leave her sleeping till I've turned on the bath-water."

She went out of the night nursery, closing the door behind her.

In a second Blinkie darted out from behind the wardrobe.

" Quick, quick ! " she gasped, " or she'll be back."

The Wicked One sprang out of bed ; Blinkie sprang in.

" It's all right, Mr. Wikky," she whispered. " It's going to be fine to-day. because the sun went to bed red, the ravens are croaking, there are cobwebs on the hedges, dew on the grass, and the smoke is rising straight from the chimney."

The Wicked One nodded his head and clapped his paws with delight.

As Nurse opened the door Blinkie saw the tip of his tail disappear beneath the window-sill as he swung himself down by the creeper.

CHAPTER VII.

THE BIRTHDAY PARTY.

"The child that is born on the Sabbath day
Is happy and blithe, and good and gay."

IT was a beautiful afternoon. The sun shone and the sky was blue.

At half-past three, half an hour before the guests were expected, Blinkie had been brought by Nurse to Hurst Woods, and told to sit on the large hamper until her friends arrived.

They came at four o'clock. The Wicked One ran in front, and directly Blinkie saw him she cried,—

"Wikky, Wikky, whatever are you carrying?"

The Wicked One had arrived with a doll's trunk dangling round his neck.

The funny old men came up as she asked the question. Mr. Why was wearing a narrow white tie, and Mr. What a broad white bow. Both had flowers in their buttonholes and white kid gloves.

" Sh - sh ! " said Mr. Why. " The Wicked One has come in fancy dress."

" That is so," observed Mr. What, sitting down on a tree-trunk, which creaked under his weight. " You must guess what he is."

" That's not very hard," Blinkie announced in a superior voice. " He's a porter."

The Wicked One jumped, squealed, and stamped with anger. He was nothing of the sort.

Blinkie wrinkled her forehead.

" He—he's Carter Paterson."

The monkey had never heard of such a person, and slashed his tail on the ground.

He ran up the tree, taking a tit-bit with him.

See page 84.

Mr. Why gave her a hint.

" He's some animal, some animal."

" Animal ? " said Blinkie, screwing up the whole of her face. " Whatever animal carries a trunk about with him ? "

Then it flashed into her mind.

" Oh, he's an elephant ! "

The Wicked One was so pleased she had at last guessed that he snatched off the trunk from round his neck and rolled it over to her feet. It opened, and out fell three presents. A bag of monkey nuts from the Wicked One, a long box of chocolates from Mr. Why, and a round box of chocolates from Mr. What.

When Blinkie had thanked each of them prettily they opened the hamper and spread the tea.

It was a good tea. The Wicked One did enjoy the icing on the birthday cake. He ran up the tree, taking a tit-bit with

him. He came down for more. He
smacked his lips. He snatched Blinkie's
cherry just as she was putting it into her
mouth ; but there were many more cher-
ries, so Blinkie did not mind.

" I *do* like birthdays," said Blinkie.
" I'd like one every week. I was born
on a Sunday, so wouldn't it be lovely if
I had a birthday every Sunday ! "

" So you were born on a Sunday ? "
said Mr. What. " It is the best day in
the week on which to be born."

" Why ? " Blinkie asked.

" Haven't you heard, haven't you heard
the little rhyme ? " said Mr. Why, smooth-
ing away the crumbs off his " party "
suit.

" What little rhyme ? "

" This little rhyme," said Mr. What.

Blinkie listened while he repeated it so
slowly that she could remember every
word.

" Monday's child is fair of face,
  Tuesday's child is full of grace,
  Wednesday's child is loving and giving,
  Thursday's child has to work for its living,
  Friday's child is full of woe,
  Saturday's child has far to go ;
  While the child that is born on the Sabbath day
  Is happy and blithe, and good and gay."

" Oh, Sunday's much the nicest ! " said
Blinkie. " I am glad I am a Sunday
girl. I'm sure Nurse must have been
born on Friday, because she's full of
woe. She's always saying she can't stoop,
because she's got a pain in her knee ; or
I mustn't make a noise, because she's got
a headache fit to split ; or cook's put too
much spice in the cake, and she can't eat
spice. Mother was born on a Saturday.
She's been ever so far away—twice to
India. Oh, it is a lovely rhyme ! " And
Blinkie said it all over again, to be sure
she had not forgotten any of it.

While they had been talking about the
rhyme the Wicked One had been very

busy. He had collected several small pieces of twig, and had laid them on the ground so that they spelt out Monday.

" Monday ? " said Blinkie. " What does he mean ? "

" He is telling you," said Mr. What, " on which day he was born."

" Oh, he's Monday's child ? " said Blinkie. " Then he is fair of face ! "

Blinkie took his little brown berry-like face between her pink hands and stroked it.

How could you call him " fair of face " when he was so dark ?

But then, perhaps, it was different in Mr. Wikky's own little world. Yes, she felt sure the Wicked One was the handsomest monkey in Monkey-land.

CHAPTER VIII.

BLINKIE FINDS OUT ALL ABOUT FATHER CHRISTMAS.

" Here come I, old Father Christmas.
Christmas or not,
I hope old Father Christmas
Will never be forgot."

WHEN Blinkie visited her old friends at Wherefore Cottage, she nearly always found them busy writing. Whenever she opened the door she would see their two heads bent over the paper they were writing on. But they were not doing so on Christmas Eve.

There was snow in the lane, and Blinkie made a straight line of footprints as she walked along it.

When she came to Wherefore Cottage

she peeped in at the parlour window. She wondered if they would roast chestnuts over the great open fire. She hoped so, for she was fond of chestnuts, and the Wicked One loved to crunch the baked skins between his strong white teeth.

The door was not bolted, so she lifted the latch and walked in.

Usually she heard, " Scratch, scratch, scratch," as the pens flew over the paper. This afternoon she heard, " Click, click, click ! "

Then Mr. Why said,—

" One purl, one plain ; knit two together. Come along in, come along in, Little Dear."

And Mr. What said,—

" Fourteen . . . Fifteen . . . Take off your pretty red coat, Miss Blinkie, and put your hat on the chair."

The Wicked One took hold of a big

ball of wool and threw it so that it hit
her on the tip of her tilted nose, for
which naughty trick he was given two
smacks from Mr. Why and a smack from
Mr. What.

When Blinkie had taken off her outdoor things and smoothed down her black
velvet frock, she ran to the fire, and perch-
ing herself on the arm of Mr. What's
chair, began to pelt the old men with
questions.

"What are you doing ?   You're making
a stocking. Oh, and you're knitting the
foot, Mr. What, and Mr. Why is knitting
the top of the leg.   But what a big stocking !   Whoever can it be for ? "

"It's for you, Little Dear, for you,
Little Dear," smiled Mr. Why.

"For me ? " said Blinkie. "But I
could almost get myself inside it as well
as my foot. It's big enough to hold a
doll's house."

The quaint little couple trotted up the frosty lane.

See page 99.

" There might be a doll's house in it to-morrow morning," said Mr. What.

" Who pays a visit to good children, to very good children, to-night ? " asked Mr. Why.

Then Blinkie knew that her kind old friends, knowing she wanted a doll's house, were knitting her a stocking big enough to hold it, should Santa Claus happen to bring her one.

" Thank you ever so much ! " she said. " Oh, I do hope Santa Claus will bring me a doll's house. I want it to be three storeys high, and to have a blue front door with a white knob handle. Last year Father Christmas brought me a teddy-bear. I wonder why he comes, and is so kind ? "

" You do not know who he is and why he comes ? " said Mr. Why, laying down his knitting, for he had finished the top of the stocking. " Shall I tell you how Santa Claus first started to visit good little boys and girls and give them lovely presents ? "

Of course Blinkie wanted to hear.

" Tell me—tell me all about Santa Claus."

Mr. Why settled in a big armchair to tell the story, while Mr. What, also in a big armchair, continued to knit the stocking. The Wicked One fetched a big paper bag. There were chestnuts inside it.

As he took them between his paws and placed them on the bars he looked up at Blinkie as much as to say : " They'll be cooked to a turn by the time the tale is told."

Mr. Why had cleared his throat to start.

" Did you ever hear, Little Dear, of a baby standing up in his bath when he was only a fortnight old ? "

" Never ! " said Blinkie, who often saw her little cousin bathed. She was six

months old, and Nurse had to hold her
lest she should slip.

"Well, this was what happened to St.
Nicholas. All his friends thought it so
wonderful that they decided he was not
like other babies, but would grow up to
be a very famous man."

"But it's Santa Claus who brings us
toys," said Blinkie, "not St. Nicholas."

"They are one and the same, one and
the same," corrected Mr. Why; "just as
Santa Claus and Father Christmas are one
and the same. Of course, Little Dear,"
he continued, "you know the story of St.
Nicholas and the cruel butcher?"

"I read it yesterday," said Blinkie.
"There was a butcher who cut up three
little boys and put them in a tub to pickle
them, and after seven years St. Nicholas
dreamed they were in the tub, and went
to the butcher's house dressed up as a
traveller."

" That's it, that's it ! " said Mr. Why.

" And when he touched the lid of the tub," Blinkie continued, " the three little boys came out none the worse for their seven years in pickle."

" St. Nicholas was glad to have saved the little boys," Mr. Why continued, "because he was very fond of children, and loved giving them presents. He loved best to give them secretly, to open the cottage door and put a bag of lollipops on the hearth, so that no one knew from whom it came.

" Once there was a poor girl who, although she was the daughter of a noble-man, could not marry because she had no money to buy a wedding-dress. St. Nicholas was very sorry for her, and flung a bag of gold through the open window of her room. A few nights later he flung a second bag in through the window, and a few nights after that a third bag of gold, which fell on to her knee. The girl's father, who had been watching from behind the door, saw St. Nicholas. He ran after him, clutched hold of his robes, and thanked him. He begged him to tell his name.

" 'I am St. Nicholas,' he answered. 'But you must promise never to speak to any one of my visits, because I like best to give my presents in secret.'

"The story, however, leaked out, and from that time onwards St. Nicholas was known as the friend of little children. All over the world little dears, little dears like yourself, learnt to love St. Nicholas. In Holland the boys and girls call him Sannik'lass for short."

" St. Nicholas—Sannik'lass ! " repeated Blinkie. " Now I see how he got the name of Santa Claus. And does he bring secret presents to the boys and girls in Holland just like he does to us at Christmas-time ? "

Mr. Why smiled over his spectacles.

" Yes, yes, Little Dear. He comes riding through Holland on a horse loaded with presents. The Dutch boys and girls put their wooden shoes under the chimney instead of hanging up their stockings like the little dears in England. They fill them with carrots and hay for Sannik'lass's horse."

" Does he tie up his horse outside the house when he takes in the presents ? " asked Blinkie.

" No, no, Little Dear ; he has a Black Boy to hold it for him. The Dutch children do not love this Black Boy, for all the year round he hides in the chimney, so that he can tell Santa Claus who have been good and who have been naughty boys and girls. Woe betide the naughty boys and girls ! " Mr. Why shook his head. " In the morning they will find birch rods in their wooden shoes, while the good ones will find many beautiful presents."

" Oh," said Blinkie, " that's just like us. If we're good, Mr. Santa Claus fills our stockings with presents ; if we are naughty, he leaves them empty."

" There, Miss Blinkie," said Mr. What, " I've finished your stocking."

" I'm quite sure," exclaimed Blinkie, " it's big enough, isn't it, to hold a doll's house three storeys high ! "

When the chestnuts had popped and been eaten, it was time for Blinkie to go home.

She put on her coat and hat, kissed Mr. Why and Mr. What, and thanked them for a nice afternoon.

" Now, Little Dear," said Mr. Why, " the Wicked One shall carry your stocking home for you."   Mr. Why folded it up and laid it across the monkey's paws.

" You'll come in and see us to-morrow ? " said Mr. What.

" Oh yes ! " said Blinkie.   " I'll be in
as early as I can to wish you a Merry,
Merry Christmas."

Mr. Why and Mr. What watched the
quaint little couple trotting up the frosty
lane. Blinkie was so funny. She felt
like the Princess in her fairy-book who
always had a page to attend on her.
So she walked with her head very high
and her back very straight, looking as
" Princessy " as she could, while the
Wicked One strutted behind holding up
the great big stocking.

" Oh, the Little Dear, the Little Dear ! "
said Mr. Why, wiping two tears out of
his faded blue eyes.

" I hope she will like the doll's house
Santa Claus is going to send her," said
Mr. What.

" It is three storeys high," said Mr.
Why, " three storeys high."

" And it has a blue front door with a

white knob handle," said Mr. What. " Now," he said, " we will hang up the mistletoe."

He moved away, but Mr. Why remained by the window.

" The bells—the bells ! "

Across the hill, down the snow-laden pathway, came the echo of the bells.

" Ding-dong ! ding-dong ! "

Mr. Why pulled the patchwork curtains.

" May the Little Dear, the Little Dear have a very happy Christmas," he said slowly.

Mr. What, although he could not speak because he had a piece of string in his mouth to tie up the mistletoe, had the same wish for Blinkie filling his great big bulging heart.

OLD NATURE TALES

HOW THE BLADDER CAMPION GOT ITS NAME

I

You no doubt have noticed it often when out for a ramble—a tall, white flower, its bell-shaped head drooping as it sways in the breeze. It is the Bladder Campion, and if you are able to distinguish the flower you may have wondered how it got its name. Shall I tell you?

Its story goes back to a time when things were very different from what we find them nowadays. In those far-off times people held what is sometimes described as " primitive beliefs," that is, they believed many things which nowadays we have ceased to regard seriously. Our ancient forefathers had a firm belief in creatures such as gnomes, fairies, spirits, and water kelpies. Nowadays most boys and girls merely laugh when such things are mentioned, which fact goes to show that a great change has taken place during the centuries in the manner in which people think.

While we worship one God, the Creator of all things, the ancients believed in quite a large number of gods and goddesses. Among those exalted beings the wisest was Minerva, and it is with her, the goddess of wisdom, that the story of the Bladder Campion is associated.

Minerva's favourite pets were said to have been owls. They were found everywhere in her palace—in the great halls, in the rooms of state, even in her sleeping apartments. When she walked out in the dusk her pets accompanied her, and flying overhead in dense masses they appeared like a giant cloud in the sky. After a time, through close association with the wise goddess, the owls' expression began to change, until at last it became fixed in that solemn stare which all owls possess even in our own day.

Owls, like other creatures that fly by night, are fond of insects, and Minerva began to find the problem of providing her pets with their favourite food a very trying one. Strive as they might, her servants never seemed able to gather sufficient flies to feed their mistress's huge brood, and being busy in other ways Minerva was not able to give as much attention to her pets as she would have liked. She became greatly grieved over their lack of suitable food, and was on the point of sending the entire flight back to their native forests to fend for themselves when her anxiety was dispelled in an unexpected way.

II

One day a ragged little boy with a shock of red hair knocked at one of the outer gates and asked to be allowed to see Minerva. The gatekeeper, seeing the boy ill-clad, and being perhaps a little suspicious as to his intentions, refused the request and ordered him away.

But the boy was persistent. "Minerva is sad," said he, "because her owls cannot be fed. I have come to feed her owls so that she may be sad no longer."

The goddess herself, who chanced to be passing at the moment, overheard the words.

A little boy knocked at one of the outer gates.

" Who is this boy," she asked, " who is come to my palace to tell me how my owls may be fed ? By what means does he intend to supply them with the flies they want ? "

Before the gatekeeper could reply, the boy stepped forward, and bowing low, said :

" I have come, O great Minerva, to request that I may be permitted to be thy devoted slave. My name is Campion. I am the son of a poor woodcutter in yonder forest, and having heard that thy servants are unable to provide sufficient flies for thine owls I have come to offer my services."

" If you can convince me," said Minerva, " that you are able to provide flies for my starving owls, I will employ you right gladly and pay you handsomely for your work."

Campion thereupon produced a large

bladder, and fixing it to the end of the long stick he carried, said :

" I crave only one chance, O great goddess. Let me show thee my skill in capturing flies with this bladder, and if I fail to provide for the needs of thine owls before nightfall I shall turn my back upon thy gates for ever."

Minerva, greatly pleased at the boy's pluck, consented at once.

" Should you succeed," she cried, " great fortune is yours ; but should you fail "—and her brow clouded—" you shall dearly rue ! "

Campion paid little attention to the goddess's threat, so eager was he to be away to the forest to capture all the flies he could find. He had spent all his life in capturing flies for his father's pet owls, and was highly skilled at his work. Therefore the task demanded by Minerva appeared so easy that he jumped for sheer joy, and waving his bladder above his head he raced away to the forest on the quest that was to bring him fortune.

At dusk he returned, carrying in a sack a huge number of flies he had captured. You can imagine with what hooting and flapping of wings he was greeted when he walked into the courtyard and released his booty. The great brown birds, issuing from their roosting places, darted with lightning movements hither and thither, revelling in the unusual feast provided for them and almost knocking Campion over in their eagerness to satisfy their hunger.

Minerva, delighted at the boy's skill, called him to her, and, smiling graciously, admitted him as a member of her household.

"You are indeed a clever lad," she said. "You have done a wonderful work this day in that you have provided sufficient food for my owls, whereas my servants have failed miserably. Henceforward you shall forget your poverty and become rich. Those rags in which you are clothed shall be thrown away, and you shall be dressed in fine silk as befits a servant of Minerva's court."

Thus the poor woodcutter's son was raised in one brief day from poverty to riches and became an important personage, so much so that his former neighbours saluted him with respect each day as he passed on a gaily caparisoned horse on his way to the forest.

III

But, as often happens even to grown-up people who have become suddenly rich, Campion grew lazy. He ate and slept too much, and spent the greater part of the time that ought to have been occupied at his work in playing games with other idlers of the court. Worst of all, he began to dislike his task of catching flies, thinking it no doubt beneath the dignity of a youth so important and so beautifully dressed as himself.

His neglect, of course, resulted in the owls becoming very thin and starved, but however much they hooted and grumbled Campion paid no attention. He continued to sleep and play games while the flies and gnats buzzed safely over his head.

At length a tale bearer carried the news to Minerva. He told her how Campion idled away his time while the owls, half starved through lack of food, were growing thinner each day, and many had in fact died.

As was to be expected, Minerva was exceedingly angry. She summoned Cam-

pion to her presence, and reprimanded
him severely, saying in conclusion :

" Although I am loth to deal harshly
with you, because you have proved yourself to be a clever lad, yet will I on no
account have an unfaithful servant in my
household.   Know, therefore, that although you are forgiven on this occasion,
you shall by no means escape punishment
should I hear again of your shirking your
duty and neglecting to feed my owls."

You may be sure it was with a thankful
heart that Campion left Minerva's presence. He felt grateful to the goddess for
not visiting dire punishment upon him,
for despite her great wisdom the goddess,
when occasion demanded, could be harsh
and even cruel. Determined, therefore,
to be more diligent in future, Campion
entered again upon his work with a new
resolve.

For a time all went well. Campion,

with bladder on stick, captured each day a vast number of flies, and Minerva's owls fared sumptuously. They grew sleek and well conditioned, and Campion, now sprightly and alert, sang at his work and forgot that ever he had been lazy. So every one was happy.

IV

Alas, however, for Campion's newly found zeal! It did not long continue, and this time his fall proved to be his undoing.

One day on his return from the forest he was met by a servant of the household who spoke to him in this wise :

" Thou art weary after thy day's labour, Campion, and thy face is pale through overmuch work. See, here is sparkling wine ; it will revive thee and cause thy

face to glow with new health. Take it ;
it is for thy good."

Campion foolishly listened to the tempter
and drank the wine. Soon from the effects
of fatigue and the powerful fumes he fell
fast asleep. He did not awaken until the
sun next day had climbed high into the
heavens, and still feeling tired and fuddled
he went about his work in a very ill-temper.
That day he caught but few flies, and the
owls hooted in anger at their meagre
rations.

The following day the same thing again
happened, for Campion, still feeling tired
and out of sorts, had drunk more wine
overnight. All day long he was in a very
confused state and did not bother about
the owls.

By-and-by the birds began to grow thin
and weakly, for Campion continued to
drink more and more wine and become
lazier every day. Forgetting the goddess's

threat, he spent the greater part of the day asleep under some shady tree in the forest ; his nights he passed in revelry with other youths as foolish as himself. He did not appear to care what happened either to himself or to the owls under his charge so long as he was able to enjoy the company of his evil companions and get plenty of wine to drink.

V

But such conduct could only end in punishment, and Campion's day of reckoning was at hand. Minerva's wrath on hearing of the lad's misconduct was terrible to behold. She ordered him sternly from her presence.

" See'st thou yonder hill," she said, pointing with her hand, " where no trees grow, only shrubs and weeds ? Hasten

She ordered him sternly from her presence.

and make thy way there, and when thou hast arrived at thy journey's end thou shalt know the fate that is in store for thee."

With dejected mien Campion left the goddess's presence, this time for ever, and with his bladder and stick over his shoulder started out on his journey as Minerva had commanded. All day long he walked, wondering the while what terrible punishment awaited him on the bare hillside towards which he was going. But he had not much more time left in which to wonder. Towards dusk, while he was toiling painfully up the face of the hill, he became suddenly transfixed, and next instant he found himself changed into the flower we know now as the Bladder Campion.

There he stands even at the present day. He is usually found on bare hillsides and in out of the way places, waving for-

lornly his empty bladder in which no flies are ever imprisoned. And if you stop and look you will notice that the flower hangs its head as it sways in the breeze.

HOW THE POPPY GREW

I

THE opium poppy is often thought of as the black sheep of the flower family; and yet every poppy, according to tradition, bears the mark of the Holy Cross in its centre. The poppy you see among the wheat is not the opium poppy. It is quite harmless, and all that can be said against it is that it is a nuisance to the farmer. Many legends have been woven around the poppy. One is a story about the postimani, or opium poppy.

A certain famous magician, while bathing one day in India's holy river, the Ganges, saw swimming towards him a tiny mouse. This mouse was unlike any other the magician had ever seen. Instead of the familiar dun-coloured coat and grey eyes, its fur was of a bright red colour. Eyes, claws, nose, all were of the same vivid hue. The astonished magician having succeeded in capturing the little creature, took it home with him and cared for it, and by-and-by it became his constant companion, following him everywhere he went.

For many years the mouse lived happily with its master ; but after a time it grew to be unhappy, and said to the magician :

" I am tired of being a mouse. I want to be something bigger and grander. If thou but speak the magic word I shall be changed and live happily for ever."

So yielding to the mouse's entreaties the magician spoke the magic word, and instantly the mouse became transformed into a cat.

Again for a time it lived contentedly with its master, but only for a time. Discontent once more took possession of it, and day and night it besought the magician to change it into something else, since it had grown tired of being a cat. So the magician changed it into a dog.

As a dog it was still unhappy, and by-and-by it was transformed into an ape, and eventually it became a bear.

But nothing the magician could do was of any avail ; the mouse still fretted, and pleaded for still another change.

" But speak the magic word," it said, " and I shall be changed into a beautiful girl. In that state I shall be radiant and happy. Grant me this request, and I promise thee it shall be my last."

The magician thought long and deeply, and at length he consented.

" Be thou changed into a beautiful girl ! " he cried, waving his magic wand. Instantly the little red mouse found itself once again transformed, but on this occasion into something far grander than it had ever been before.

" I name thee Postimani," said the magician, " and among all the maids of the East thou shalt be fairest."

Then, and only then, was the little red mouse content.

II

One day as Postimani was gathering flowers in the fields, the king of that country rode by.

" Ho ! " he cried, drawing rein, " whom have we here ? A lovely maid indeed. What may thy name be, fair one ? "

As Postimani spoke her name her voice sounded like sweet music in the king's ears.

" And who are thy parents ? " he asked, bewitched by her beauty.

Now Postimani, partly through fear,

but largely urged by ambition, lied to the king.

"My father," she said, "was a prince of a far-distant country, but when a child I was carried away by robbers, and I never saw him again. I was found wandering by a good, kind magician who adopted me as his own daughter, and I have lived with him here ever since."

"Then, by my sooth," cried the king, "thou shalt live with him no longer. This day shalt thou accompany me to my palace, where thou shalt sit on my right hand, and be queen of all my realm."

So Postimani went to the king's palace and reigned as his queen. And they lived happily together many years.

As time went on it was noticed that Postimani's beauty, unlike that of other women, did not fade, but grew even more radiant with the passing years. Her fame spread abroad, and people journeyed from

" What may thy name be, fair one ? "

See page 121.

distant parts of the country eager to obtain even a fleeting glimpse of their beautiful queen.

But as Postimani grew more beautiful she also became more vain. Each day she spent long hours before her mirror, posturing, titivating, and admiring her dimpled cheeks. Then one day a terrible thing happened.

Walking alone in the courtyard of the palace, Postimani paused at the brink of a deep well to gaze into the depths. She was surprised to see how clearly her features were reflected ; every lineament was mirrored distinctly ; her auburn hair shone like a golden aureole in the still water. It was wonderful—far surpassing the most perfect mirror the queen had ever seen.

Turning away at last she suddenly became dizzy. Her foot slipped, and she clutched vainly at the ledges for support.

But her grasp was not sufficiently strong to save her, and she fell to the bottom.

III

Great was the grief at court when it became known that Postimani was missing. The king wept bitterly, and would not be comforted. " Gold ! " he cried, " gold and silver will I give him who shall restore my queen unto me ! " But the searchers returned sadly, each with the same tale. Queen Postimani could not be found.

At length there appeared before the palace gate an old, bowed man who demanded an audience of the king. It was the magician. When asked his business he replied, " I bear tidings of Postimani. Go, tell your master that I tarry at the gate." On hearing this the servants hastened to deliver the message, and the magician was admitted to the presence of the king.

There the old man told the king of the fate that had befallen his wife. But he told also the true story of the beautiful queen : how she had deceived him, and the many changes through which she had been transformed. And as the king listened his former grief was turned to anger.

" Let her body remain where it lies," he commanded, " and fill the well to the brim. Thus shall the memory of Posti-mani be forgotten ! "

Next morning as the king, walking early, passed by the site of the well he beheld a strange thing. From amid the heap of earth and stones there had grown overnight a great mass of bloom which now swayed and danced in the morning breeze. It was the poppy, afterwards named the postimani, and from that

eastern courtyard it has spread until now varieties of it are found in nearly every country of the world.

The legend adds a word of caution. Whoever tastes the seed of the poppy undergoes, like Queen Postimani, certain transformations, and develops a quality of each of the animals into which the little red mouse had been changed. Thus, one would first become timid like a mouse, then fond of hunting like a cat, fierce as a dog, mischievous as an ape, surly as a bear, and all the time would be discontented like Queen Postimani herself.

WHY THE SEA IS SALT

I

THERE are many different versions of the story telling how the sea became salt, and each country has its own version. This is the Norse legend :

There were two brothers, one rich and the other poor. It was Christmas Eve, and the poor man's wife said to her husband, " We have nothing in the house with which to keep Christmas. Go and

beg food from your brother, for he has
enough and to spare, and we shall be
merry and invite our neighbours to join
us."

So the poor man set out on the journey,
and did not stop until he came to his rich
brother's house.

" My wife and I cannot keep Christmas," he said, " for our meal is finished
and we haven't a crust in the cupboard.
Give me food to carry home with me,
brother, that we may eat and not starve."

But the rich brother was a hard, worldly
man ; he did not wish to have poor relations calling at his fine mansion.

" I will give you a leg of venison," said
he, " if you promise to do what I shall
ask you to."

His brother, thinking of his empty cupboard and hungry wife, consented.

" Here then," said the rich brother, " is
your leg of venison. Now, you will kindly

leave my house and go straight to the realm of Loki."

The poor brother stood aghast. The grim underworld of which he had heard so much, lay away somewhere in the dark spaces, he did not know where. Neither did he know any one who could tell him the way thither.

But his rich brother would not listen to any objection.

" A promise is a promise," said he. " Get you gone at once."

" Very well," said the poor man at length. " I have given my word, and I expect I shall have to keep it. I don't know where Loki's realm is, but I suppose I shall get there sometime."

So he lifted the leg of venison on to his shoulder and set out.

After walking for some hours in a straight direction he began to feel tired and sat down to rest. He noticed that it had begun to grow dark, and that the appearance of the country had changed. As he sat by the roadside an old man passed along carrying a bundle of sticks he had gathered for his Christmas fire. He had a long white beard reaching to his waist, and shouted a cheerful greeting.

" Good-evening, friend ! " said the old man. " Whither are you bound this Christmas Eve ? "

" Good-evening to you, old man," said the other, returning the greeting. " I am going to the realm of Loki ; but where it is I know not. Perhaps you may be able to direct me thither ? "

" That I shall," said the old man promptly, " and with little trouble too, for you are there already."

" Indeed ! " said the man with the leg of venison. " I am surprised. I thought it would be ever so much darker."

" Well, well," said the old man, " per-

"Whither are you bound this Christmas Eve?"

haps you did ; but it isn't as black as it's painted. Now, the king's palace is just across the way. I should advise you to sell His Majesty that beautiful leg of venison. He is very fond of venison, and will pay you any money you ask. But take my advice and don't part with your venison for money ; insist on having the quern which you will see just inside the outer door."

The poor man thanked his newly found friend and rose and went on his way to the palace.

" If you obtain the quern," shouted the old man after him, " come to me and I will show you how it works."

So he went on and soon he was admitted to the presence of the king.

He had no sooner entered the palace than a crowd of courtiers swarmed up to him, eager to buy his leg of venison, and each trying to outbid the other. So great

was the din that the king at length demanded silence.

"You have come to sell your venison,"
said he, addressing the poor man. "Very
well. Since venison is my favourite dish
you will be paid any money you ask. You
have only to name your price."

"May it please your Majesty," said the
poor man, "I'd rather not accept money.
Instead, should your Majesty be willing,
I'd take the hand quern which I noticed
behind the door yonder."

The king at first was very unwilling to
part with the quern, and haggled with the
man for a long time, but the latter stuck
to what he had said, and at length the king
gave way.

"Take the quern, then," he cried in a
great rage, "and get you gone."

II

The poor man took the quern and reaching the highway found the old man with the long white beard awaiting him. The friendly woodcutter showed him how to handle the quern and said, " Your fortune is surely made, for it is good to grind almost anything."

The poor man thanked his informant, and set off for home, running at top speed. So quickly did he run that each mile seemed but a few yards, and when he came to his own door the village clock was chiming the hour of midnight.

His wife, sitting up awaiting his coming, was very cross. " You're a fine husband," she scolded. " Wherever have you been so late ? I've been waiting for you hour after hour, with no food to eat and not a stick to put on the fire."

" Oh," said the husband, " I've been here and I've been there, and I couldn't get back earlier. But I've brought something with me which will open your eyes with astonishment. Just hold your tongue and watch."

Thereupon he placed the quern on the table and bade it grind out food and drink and firewood. To the astonishment of the wife the quern did as it had been bidden. Soon the place was overflowing with the best food and drink, and a great fire blazed in the fireplace. You may be sure that when the pair went to bed that night they were happier than ever they had been in their lives.

Next day they decided to give a feast to all their neighbours and relations. The quern ground out dainties of every description, and not only that, but also gold and silver plate, tapestries, and beautiful furnishing. When the guests arrived they gazed in wonderment at the splendour around them.

" Only yesterday," they said, " they hadn't even a fire in the grate ; now their house is more magnificent than the king's palace."

Among the guests was the rich brother. He had never seen such grandeur before, and could hardly believe his eyes. But his brother would not let him into the secret, though he begged him almost with tears to tell him where he had obtained his sudden riches. He was a greedy man, that brother, and the sight of so much plenty made him wish to get hold of it for himself.

At last, while the two brothers sat drinking wine, the secret was revealed. The owner of the quern told the other of his journey to the underworld, and of his wonderful discovery there. The brother listened to his story and determined there and then to obtain possession of the quern for himself. He offered large sums of money, but the owner of the quern always refused.

" My price," he said at length, " is twenty thousand pounds. Pay me my price, and the quern is yours."

The rich brother, glad to obtain such a valuable article at any price, paid over the money and took the quern home with him.

His trade was that of a fish merchant, and, above everything else, he wanted fish and still more fish. So he set the quern to grind salmon, the finest fish of all.

Large and small, fresh and silvery from the sea they came in their thousands, so many, indeed, that in a short space of time the house was full to overflowing. Still the quern went on grinding, and still the number of salmon grew until at length the rich man was forced to flee from his house. He ran down the road with the salmon flowing in a great stream behind him, and never stopped until he had reached his brother's door.

"Take back your quern!" he cried. "The thing is bewitched; it won't stop grinding out fish. Take it away at once, or my house will be ruined."

His brother sat back in his chair and laughed until his sides ached. He had expected this to happen, for although he had told his brother how to make the quern grind things, he had been careful not to tell him how to make it stop.

"Ho, ho!" he laughed. "That's a fine joke. What a funny fellow you are, to be sure; but I shan't take the quern back unless you promise to pay me another ten thousand pounds."

"Very well," replied his brother, "I will pay you the money with pleasure. Only come at once and remove the quern. I never want to see it again."

So the quern was brought back, and the fish merchant was left with tons upon tons of salmon which he would never be able to sell.

III

The owner of the quern became, of course, very rich. He built for himself a fine house overlooking the sea ; the walls were hung with gold and silver plate which glittered in the sun and caused the crews of passing vessels to gaze in astonishment.

One day the captain of a strange ship chanced to see the splendid glitter. He had never seen such a fine mansion anywhere, and decided to go ashore and pay his respects to the owner. He was most kindly received, and a great feast was prepared for the entire crew.

Later the captain was shown the wonderful quern ; he was told that it was the source of all the wealth and grandeur he had seen.

" It will grind out almost anything," said the owner with much pride. " Gold and silver, food and drink, shoes and clothing—everything, in fact, that a man or woman needs."

" Can it grind salt ? " inquired the captain. He traded in salt, and often made long, risky voyages across the seas to obtain it. " Now," he thought, " if only I can obtain this quern my fortune is made."

" You shall see it grinding out salt this instant," said the other, and without more ado he placed the quern on the table. Immediately it began to grind out a stream of fine white salt.

" Marvellous ! " said the captain. " Are you willing to sell your wonderful quern ? "

" Oh yes," said his host, smiling at the

thought of the bargain he had made with his brother. " I am perfectly willing to sell my quern—for ten thousand pounds ! "

" That's a lot of money," said the captain thoughtfully. " Nevertheless I must have salt—as much as I can get. It will save me many a dangerous voyage across the ocean."

So he paid the money and carried the quern away with him to his ship.

When he had sailed a long way off he brought the quern on deck and bade it work.

" Grind salt," he cried, " and grind both good and fast ! "

The quern at once obeyed. It ground out a stream of salt that overran the deck and poured into the ship's holds. Soon the vessel was so heavily burdened that it came to a standstill ; but the quern kept on grinding, for nobody knew how to stop it, and still the volume of salt grew.

At last the ship began to sink, and the captain and his men put off in their boats. They had just time to get clear when the laden ship sank, carrying with it the quern, still busy grinding out salt.

Sailors passing near the spot in calm weather say they can hear the quern grinding on the ocean bed. It is busy still at its task, and that is the reason—so they say—why the sea is salt !

WHY THE COCK CROWS AT DAWN

WHY does a cock crow at break of day?
You don't know? Well, here's the story.
It begins " once upon a time," as all good
stories should.

Once upon a time the world was very
young—just as you are now. The only
light that reached the earth came from the
moon and the stars at night. There was
no sun, so that during the day everything
was in darkness.

There were no men and women living on the earth then, but giant beasts roamed through the forests, and great birds flew with a terrific swish of wings through the air. You wouldn't have liked to live in those far-off times, I'm sure, because everything was all jumbled up, so to speak, and dreadful things were always happening.

Well, it happened one day while Acram the heron was sitting on her nest that who should come that way but Rocus the rook. In the darkness he didn't notice the heron sitting there, and, in any case, he had no time to prevent an accident. Next instant he had barged into Acram with such force that she was thrown off her nest.

" Take care, can't you ! " squawked the heron in a great rage. " You're an impudent fellow ! What do you mean by knocking me off my eggs in this fashion ? "

" Get out of my way ! " cawed the rook. " You're only a great, clumsy water-fowl ! You'd no business to be sitting in my path anyway."

Then Acram and Rocus quarrelled until they began to fight. The heron, being bigger, was the stronger of the two, but the rook was more nimble and found no difficulty in keeping out of reach of his pursuer. After a time he grew tired of being chased and flew into a tree-top, and from there flung bitter taunts at Acram, who was unable to follow him.

The heron, listening to Rocus's jeers, became more angry still, and would have killed the rook could she have caught him. With her heavy body and webbed feet she could not fly into the tree-top, but if only she could find a stone, she thought, she might be able to hit her tormentor. She searched for long enough, but alas ! there was no pebble to be found anywhere.

Giant beasts roamed through the forests.

At length, in despair, she went to her nest and taking up an egg aimed it at Rocus. The little black fellow ducked, and the egg went soaring into the sky.

Acram had thrown it with such force that it travelled for miles and miles ; it might, indeed, have been travelling now had it not chanced to hit a great mountain of twigs which stood in the sky right in its way. It broke, and the yolk was scattered over part of the kindling.

Immediately the great pile began to burn. The fire caught slowly at first. Gradually it gained strength, and at midday it was a blazing furnace. Living creatures on the earth gazed up at it in astonishment. They were able for the first time to see objects clearly, and beheld rivers and streams, mountains and seas, and a world of which they scarcely knew anything. In many places they had to seek shelter, so great was the heat given forth by the blazing pile high in the heavens.

Towards evening the heat became gradually less intense. The mass of firewood was burning down, and a few hours later it had burned out altogether. Then darkness came down as before.

Now, the dwellers in the heavens had also noticed the great blaze, and the Good Spirit who rules the air looked down and saw how beautiful the earth appeared in the ruddy glow. So he called the lesser spirits, his servants, together, and said, " See how beautiful the earth looks beneath the glow of yonder blazing pile. Light has appeared where before there was but darkness, and all creatures rejoice. Therefore I command that each day a great fire be lit in the heavens, so that there may be light on the face of the earth."

And the lesser spirits answered, " Thou

hast commanded, Good Master. So let
it be ! "

Every morning since then the servants
of the Good Spirit set the kindling alight.
At first it burns slowly, but afterwards
when the pile is completely aglow the
heat is very great. Then it dies down
until only the embers are left. These are
wrapped up by the clouds and used again
for lighting the fire on the morrow.

When it is nearly time for the fire to be
lit the spirits send out the morning star.
It is a warning to all creatures to be ready
to greet the first rays of the Great Fire
which now we know as the sun.

But as time went on it was found that
many lay abed. Either they were too
lazy to get up, or else so sound asleep that
they could not be wakened by the shining
star. The spirits, therefore, decided to
send a herald to awaken the sleeping
world.

They met and debated among themselves who should be appointed to the high office. But although they sat for long hours and talked about the matter for many days they were not able to decide. Then one day, as they sat talking, the crowing of a cock was heard.

"Our difficulty is solved at last!" cried one. "Let's ask chanticleer. He has a loud, shrill voice, as you have just heard. We cannot get a better or louder herald anywhere."

So the farmyard cock was brought in and offered the post of Herald of the Dawn. He was told that his only duty would be to crow aloud at daybreak. All creatures asleep would thus be warned to prepare to greet the first rays of light.

"And should you ever fail us," said the spirits, "we should not again light the Great Fire, but would leave the world to return to its former darkness."

On hearing these words the cock consented at once.

" If by my crowing," he said, " I can save the world from darkness, then I shall crow at every dawn till the end of time."

And from that day till now chanticleer has been Herald of the Dawn. Sometimes you may perhaps lie awake in the early morning listening to his cock-a-doodle-doo and wondering what he is saying. In his own language he is saying just this :

" The spirits are lighting the Great Fire. Get up, get up ! "

THE GREAT BEAR AND
THE LITTLE BEAR

I

THE sky is beautifully clear to-night, and the stars are a wonderful sight. There's no mistaking the Plough or Great Bear, and snuggling into it is the Little Bear. Its tail is like a row of diamonds!

You will wonder, no doubt, how the names Great and Little Bear came to be given to heavenly bodies, but it's all told in an old, old story almost as old as the hills. Here is the story:

Once there lived a king of Arcadia who had a beautiful daughter. The name of this princess was Callisto, and she was

Callisto was renowned as a horsewoman.

said to be the most beautiful maiden in all her father's dominions.

As Callisto grew up she became very fond of hunting, and was renowned as a horsewoman. With a few specially chosen companions of her own age she ventured into the deepest forests where wild animals abounded, and such was her skill that she was never known to return to her father's palace without bringing with her many trophies of the chase.

And how the courtiers fawned on her! Crowding round her they would whisper sweet words secretly, or, more often still, shout their admiration in a loud voice so that all might hear, " Bravo, Callisto ! "

It was a happy court and a contented country over which the king reigned. But the old monarch found his real happiness not in the pomp and splendour of state but rather in the simple joys of his home, where Callisto was the presiding star.

Now it happened that Arcadia was often visited by another huntress, a personage much more renowned than even the king's daughter. She was, in fact, none other than the famous Diana, the goddess of hunting, and the most wonderful huntress in the world.

Away in the mountains, deep in the forests, afar on the broad meadow lands her horn could be heard ; yet the elusive Diana and her bodyguard of maidens hunted unseen. No eye beheld them as they rode out in the flush of the morning, each armed with a spear and bow, and each with a quiver in which a score of silver arrows rattled as the prancing horses dashed forward, fleet as the wind. None saw them at noontide when they sought the shade of some leafy grove, where they bathed in the cool stream ; or, it may have been, when they danced under the great evergreen trees while their merry laughter rang loud and long through the forest. At nightfall, returning home, the clank of galloping hooves might be heard in the distance, but the sound came only faintly, borne from faraway horizons where few dared to follow.

Sometimes a hunter of the king's court, more daring than the rest, would endeavour to spy upon the goddess and her maidens as they hunted or disported themselves in play. But such rashness met with quick punishment, and none ever returned to tell what he had seen.

Terrible stories were told of Diana's anger and cruelty, and of her power to change men into animals and other living creatures. Once a comely knight, noted for his daring and skill in the hunting field, hearing the goddess and her train pass, followed. He overtook them as they dismounted to bathe in a shaded pool, and such was Diana's wrath that she

changed the unfortunate youth instantly
into a roe deer. Before he had time to
escape, his own hounds flew upon him
and tore him to pieces. After this awful
happening Diana was left to come and go
in peace.

II

The only person who lived in no fear
of the goddess was the king's daughter.
Callisto, indeed, had for long cherished a
secret ambition to join Diana's band of
maidens, and had more than once wandered alone into the mountains in the
hope of meeting with the huntresses.
Being a woman, and the king's daughter
besides, she knew Diana would do her no
harm. Indeed, Callisto hoped she might
permit her to become one of her attendants.

Then would she be perfectly happy.

Few knew the forests and mountains as intimately as she. Every lair of fox and boar was known to her, every mile of river and stream where sprightly fish leaped, or lay unseen beneath overhanging rocks. There was little that Diana could teach her, but although few secrets of the chase were hidden from her, yet to be numbered amongst the goddess's band would be for her the realization of her most glorious dream.

Life at court after all was apt to become dull at times; constant flattery wearied her, made her feel angry even. Her life lacked that complete freedom for which she had always craved and which she assured herself she would find in full measure at the court of Diana.

There she would be free to come and go, to ride a fleet steed that travelled like the wind, to place her elfin bugle to her lips and awaken echoes which would be borne far afield over streams and meadows even to her father's palace.

Her father—ah! how proud the king would be when his daughter returned from time to time to tell of her new life; of her many adventures, of days spent in hunting and of nights given up to gaiety and the dance!

Such were the thoughts that ran through her head from morning till night. Everywhere she went she carried them with her, until one day while resting alone on a mossy bank she fell asleep. She dreamt that at last she had been admitted to the court of Diana, and that the goddess had actually chosen her to be one of her bodyguard.

So real had been her dream that on awaking Callisto felt much disappointment at being brought back from the gorgeous scenes of her vision to what now appeared to her a grey, drab world. Tears began to well up in her eyes. She wiped them quickly away, but her feelings at length overcame her, and she turned her face to the soft, green earth and wept aloud.

By-and-by she heard the sound of soft footsteps approaching, and raising her head she became aware of the presence of the most beautiful lady she had ever seen. The stranger's dress was of shimmering white, and in her hand she carried a bow. A quiver was slung across her shoulders; on her head was a silver crescent. At sight of the goddess's crown Callisto instantly raised herself and bowed thrice, for she knew that she was in the presence of the great Diana herself.

" Weep not," said Diana, " for the dream you have just dreamed will this day come true. You are chosen, Callisto, to be one of my band of maidens, for I have heard of your hunting feats, and you shall be one of my chief attendant huntresses. Come with me ! "

Then did Callisto's heart leap for sheer joy, and she bowed herself again before Diana ; for you must understand that even the daughter of a king is not equal in greatness to a goddess.

And what of the long, joyous days that followed—days when Diana and her attendants hunted from dawn till nightfall, when the mountains and forests heard the sound of their horns, and the wild beasts fled before their spears or were slain as they ran ?

It was the exciting life that Callisto had always longed for ; it was to her an ideal existence. As time went on she became happier than ever she had been before as, day by day, she rode behind the fair goddess who led the way with gleaming crescent and silver arrows jingling in her quiver.

III

Now, on Mount Olympus there lived a god named Jupiter. Olympus, according to the old legends, was the abode of many gods and goddesses; but of them all, however powerful or fierce or beautiful, Jupiter was by far the most famous. He was, in fact, king of the gods. He possessed marvellous powers, and could, if he wished, transform himself from his own huge, imposing form into that of a beautiful maiden or into a beast or a bird or a handsome youth.

His queen, Juno, had also certain wonderful powers; but she was cross and bad-tempered, and spent a great deal of her time in scolding her husband. For this reason Jupiter was often away from home for long periods, for he dreaded his wife's persistent scolding and lived very unhappily.

One day, after a bitter quarrel with Juno, he descended to Arcadia. As he walked along, still sulky, suddenly he heard the sound of a hunting horn. Quickly changing himself into a bird, he soon saw Diana and her huntresses pass that way. Immediately behind the goddess rode Callisto, and so beautiful did she appear to him that Jupiter there and then determined to see her closer and speak with her.

For a long time he pondered how best this could be done, and at length he decided on a plan. He would disguise himself as Diana, so that Callisto, unaware of the deception, would speak to him without fear.

The plan succeeded even better than Jupiter had hoped. Poor Callisto, overjoyed at being asked to walk with her mistress in the woods, obeyed gladly, never for a moment dreaming that her charming companion was not the real Diana.

Together they walked across broad meadows and through shady woods, halting by rippling streams to stoop and drink. Pausing again they would pass an idle hour reclining on some green bank where wild flowers grew, until the setting sun told them of the coming of dusk.

Next day, and for many days afterwards, Jupiter came again and walked through the woods with Callisto, until at length he grew to be very fond of his young companion. He loved to listen to her innocent laughter and look upon her beautiful face, and Juno, alas! plain and ill-tempered, was almost forgotten.

Juno in the meantime had grown very uneasy regarding her lord's periods of absence from home. These of late had grown more and more frequent. She was possessed of a jealous nature and could not bear to think of Jupiter in the company of any woman except herself. So one day she decided to watch her husband's movements as he left Olympus in the cool of the evening as was his wont.

Following him to Arcadia her worst fears were realized. She saw Jupiter, in his disguise, with Callisto as they passed along quite close to where she lay hidden, and she was filled with furious jealousy. At once she set about planning revenge.

But she could not bring herself to do Jupiter any harm. He was, after all, her lord, and she was secretly proud of being the queen of the gods. She would therefore do him no ill, but rather would she try to win him back to herself, to persuade him to live with her on Mount Olympus, and to be as happy as her plain looks and ill-temper would allow. But Callisto must be punished. Her beauty would be destroyed for ever. Against her the angry Juno would take a revenge that would be swift and terrible.

IV

The following morning Callisto arose, little dreaming of the fate that lay in store for her. She went to the river as usual to bathe, but as she walked, suddenly a strange sensation shot through her body. Looking down she was horrified to see her skin covered with a coating of shaggy hair, while her former shapely fingers now appeared like claws. Shocked at the change that appeared in her, Callisto hastened to the water's edge. Looking at her reflection in the clear depths she knew at once that she had been the victim of an evil enchantment ; that she was no longer her former lovely self, but a bear—huge, ungainly, and ugly.

Her first act was to seek Diana. She would tell the goddess what had happened and beseech her for help. But Diana failed to recognize her attendant in her new shape. Seeing a bear approaching she shot an arrow at it and roused her huntresses, and soon the glades rang with the baying of hounds.

Callisto, almost frantic, tried to speak and explain. But she found to her dismay that her power of speech had gone, and that she was only able to utter deep growls. Aware now of her dire position, she turned and fled for her life before her pursuers.

All day long the chase continued. Through forests and across mountain slopes sped Callisto; behind her, with blaring horns and eager spears, followed Diana and her band, never thinking in their zest for the chase that they were hunting a loved companion. At length night came down and hid their quarry from their sight. Bleeding and trembling, Callisto dragged herself to a near-by cave, and there, alone and forsaken, she fell asleep.

Great was the grief at Diana's court when Callisto did not return. Her companions wept for her for many moons, thinking she had been devoured in the forest by wild animals or been carried away by a raging torrent. Her father, the king, also mourned for her with tears and would not listen to words of comfort.

One thing, and one only, brought some measure of comfort to the old king. Callisto had left at her father's court her little boy only a few years old. This child, now his mother had gone, became his grandfather's constant companion, riding out with him during the day and sleeping in his apartment by night.

For long, weary years Callisto lived in the woods and in caves in the mountains. From being a huntress she became the hunted, and dared not venture far from a place of safety. Sometimes when she had wandered farther than usual into the open there would come borne to her on the wind the sound of a distant horn. It was Diana riding to the chase.

Poor Callisto, thinking sadly of other days, would rush back to her cave and there crouch in the darkness until the danger had passed.

V

In the meantime Callisto's son was growing up into a fine young man. He resembled his mother in that he was fond of hunting and outdoor sports, and every year saw him growing more skilled in the use of spear and bow. He still lived at the king's palace, and loved to bring home his trophies to show to the king, his grandfather, and to the courtiers who gathered round him just as they had gathered round Callisto his mother when she returned from the hunting field.

But that was twenty long years ago. The king often grew sad when the young hunter returned with his spoils, for he was reminded of the happy days when Callisto was still with him.

One day while hunting on the mountains the young hunter became separated from his companions and wandered from the path. He tried to retrace his steps, and in so doing passed quite close to a cave to which, it so happened, Callisto was on her way.

The two came face to face on the mountain side. Callisto immediately recognized the youth, and forgetting in the joy of the moment the change that had

been wrought in her through Juno's black art, rushed eagerly forward to embrace her long lost son.

She did not stop to think what the consequences might be, and you can imagine her dismay when she saw her son level his spear and prepare to rush upon her. He, thinking he was being attacked by a furious bear, prepared to slay the animal in defence of his own life. Another instant and his spear would have pierced his mother's heart, when—well, a strange thing happened !

Jupiter, you will remember, did not live happily on Mount Olympus with Juno, and since Callisto's disappearance was away from home more often than ever. He felt very bitter towards his queen, because he thought she had hidden away his lovely companion, and during all these years he had never wearied in his search for her. He always thought of her as a graceful girl, never dreaming for a moment that his beautiful Callisto was now roaming the forests and mountains in the shape of a bear.

On the day when Callisto met her son, Jupiter had sat himself down to rest on a mountain many, many miles away. But so powerful was his vision that objects at a distance appeared close at hand. He had, therefore, no difficulty in seeing quite clearly what was happening, and as he looked he gave a sudden start. The bear all at once had become familar to him. It was his long lost Callisto !

He sprang to his feet and raised his hand. Instantly the spear borne by Callisto's son became a harmless twig, and he himself was transformed into a small bear.

Juno's spite and jealousy had at length been revealed. Jupiter stood for a long while wondering how best to make amends for the suffering his queen had brought on Callisto. He decided that she and her son should live for ever with the Immortals in the skies, and with a sweep of his great arm he snatched them both away.

There, every night when the sky is clear, you may still see them as two beautiful groups of stars. We know them as the Great Bear and the Little Bear; but I like, somehow, to think of them as Callisto, daughter of the king of Arcadia, and her little son.

THE END

PRINTED IN GREAT BRITAIN AT
THE PRESS OF THE PUBLISHERS